Blue's Clues

Blue's Big Pajama Party

by **Adam Peltzman**

illustrated by
Jenine Pontillo

Simon Spotlight/Nick Jr.

Did you see the Big Dipper? You did? Did you find all three clues too? It's time to go to the thinking chair!

Now let's think. Our clues are a lamp, a book, and a sleeping bag. So what does Blue want to do tonight? Hmm . . . we can get into our sleeping bags. And turn on the lamp—that would give us light. But what will we do with a book?

Come on, let's all get into our sleeping bags and read a book. Hey, do you see *Good Night Bird* on the shelf? It's one of Blue's favorite bedtime stories.